HAPPY HOLIDAYS!

THIS BOOK IS DEDICATED TO MY BEAUTIFUL LITTLE LOVES, ZOE AND NATHANIEL. THANK YOU FOR CHOOSING ME TO BE YOUR MUMMY.

"Is Santa real?" by Crystal Hardstaff
Published by The Gentle Counsellor

2021

Queensland, Australia

www.thegentlecounsellor.com

Copyright 2021 The Gentle Counsellor

First Edition

For any inquiries please contact Crystal Hardstaff at @thegentlecounsellor or hello@thegentlecounsellor.com

NOTES FOR THE PARENTS

You may have chosen to read this book to your child because you have already been going along with the modernised tale of Santa but have nce decided you felt uncomfortable with this, or you may have a baby or oddler and are deciding on what you want to do. The truth and magic of Santa can co-exist, as this can still enhance their wellbeing through imaginative play.

As you read this story with your child they may have different reactions depending on what they already do or do not know about Santa. This ould include excitement, confusion, relief, or disappointment. As parents d caregivers, we need to be there to support our children through all the emotions that they will experience throughout their life.

Take the time to sit and be with each other, allowing them to ask any questions and to receive comfort if needed.

Follow my 3 step strategy:

1 - Acknowledge their feelings (name their emotion)
"You're feeling confused right now."

2 - Validate their experience
t can feel strange to know that adults haven't been completely honest."

3 - Focus on connection or redirection
Iave a cuddle. "What do you think about being Santa one day like I am?"

Throughout the book you will see these red question boxes which you can use to pause and discuss with your child.

THE CLOCK TICKED PAST BEDTIME,
AS LITTLE LEGS CURLED UP IN BED.
THERE IS ALWAYS ENOUGH TIME FOR KISSES
ON TOP OF SWEET LITTLE HEADS.

A BIG YAWN IS LET OUT,
THE SIGN OF MANY MOMENTS OF PLAY.
TOMORROW WILL BRING MORE ADVENTURE
BECAUSE IT'S FINALLY CHRISTMAS DAY!

THE ROOM BECAME STILL AND QUIET
IT'S NOW TIME TO SLEEP FOR A WHILE.
"GOODNIGHT MY LITTLE DARLING,"
MUMMY SAID SOFTLY WITH A SMILE.

BUT AS SHE WALKED TOWARDS THE DOOR
TO ENJOY A QUIET MOMENT AT LAST
A LITTLE VOICE SPOKE UP
"MUMMY, IS SANTA REAL?" HE ASKED.

SHE PAUSED AND TOOK A DEEP BREATH
THEN SAT ON THE EDGE OF HIS BED.
"WHAT AN INTERESTING QUESTION YOU ASK"
REPLIED MUMMY AS SHE FELT A WAVE OF DREAD

WHAT DO YOU THINK THE ANSWER IS?
I WONDER IF YOU'VE ASKED THIS TOO.
IT'S TIME TO LISTEN CLOSE
AS WE HEAR HER POINT OF VIEW.

YOU'VE PROBABLY ALREADY NOTICED
THAT THERE'S A LOT OF SANTAS AT THE SHOPS.
YOU FIND HIM EVERYWHERE IT SEEMS
BUT HOW DOES HE MAKE ALL OF THOSE STOPS?

MAYBE YOU'VE HEARD OTHER KIDS TALKING
AND SAYING THAT IT IS JUST NOT TRUE.
SOMETIMES IT CAN FEEL HURTFUL
WHEN SOMEONE SAYS THIS TO YOU.

"YOU SURE HAVE GROWN A LOT THIS YEAR
YOU ARE TALLER AND KINDER TOO
I SEE HOW BIG YOUR HEART IS"
SHE SAID, FINALLY KNOWING WHAT TO DO.

"I AM GOING TO TELL YOU THE SANTA STORY.
I HAVE BEEN WAITING TO FINALLY SHARE
ABOUT HOW THE WHOLE WORLD FINDS JOY
IN TREATING EACH OTHER WITH CARE."

"A LONG TIME AGO,
SANTA WAS REAL LIKE YOU AND ME.
HIS NAME WAS ST NICHOLAS
AND HE GAVE TO THOSE IN NEED."

"HE BECAME A SECRET GIFT-GIVER
GOING OUT INTO THE NIGHT.
CHILDREN LEFT EMPTY BOOTS ON THE STREET
WHICH GAVE ST NICHOLAS MUCH DELIGHT.

"HE FILLED THOSE BOOTS UP
WITH SOME COINS AND TREATS."

HOW WOULD YOU FEEL
TO FIND SOMETHING SO SWEET?

"WAITING WITH ANTICIPATION
AS THE SUN ROSE OVER THE HILL
THE CHILDREN WOULD FIND SOMETHING SPECIAL
OH WHAT A THRILL!"

"THEIR FACES LIT UP WITH JOY
THE CHILDREN SMILED FROM EAR TO EAR.
WHAT A WONDERFUL THING TO DO
BRINGING THEM SO MUCH CHEER."

"ST NICHOLAS TRULY BELIEVED THAT
ALL CHILDREN ARE WORTHY AND GOOD
HE SHOWED COMPASSION, GENEROSITY AND LOVE
IN ALL THE WAYS HE COULD."

"NOWADAYS PEOPLE CALL HIM SANTA
AND LIKE TO PRETEND THAT HE IS REAL.
EVERYONE CHOOSES THEIR OWN TRADITIONS
LIKE ENJOYING A CHRISTMAS MEAL."

"WE CAN STILL PLAY SANTA
IT'S A LOT OF FUN TOO,
LIKE PRESENTS APPEARING UNDER THE TREE!"

WHAT ARE SOME TRADITIONS YOU LIKE TO DO?

"YOU KNOW HOW YOU LIKE TO PLAY DRESS UP?
ADULTS HAVE FUN DOING THIS TOO.
WHAT MATTERS MOST TO US
IS TO SHARE SOME MAGIC WITH YOU."

"IT'S FUN TO FILL UP STOCKINGS
AND LEAVE PRESENTS UNDER THE TREE.
WE HAVE FUN PRETENDING TO BE SANTA
BUT THE TRUTH IS THAT..."

"IT'S FROM DADDY AND ME."

"CAN I BE SANTA MUMMY?" HE ASKED
"CAN I BE JUST LIKE YOU?'

CAN YOU THINK OF SOME SELFLESS THINGS
THAT YOU WOULD LIKE TO DO?

"WE ALL CAN DO SANTA'S JOB YOU SEE,
THERE ARE SO MANY THINGS TO THINK OF.
EVERYONE CAN HELP SPREAD HIS MESSAGE
OF CHEER, HOPE, SPIRIT AND LOVE."

"SANTA LIVES IN ALL OUR HEARTS
AND PERHAPS YOU MAY JUST FIND
THAT YOU CAN BECOME HIM TOO
WHEN YOU DO SOMETHING KIND."

"CHRISTMAS IS ABOUT HELPING OTHERS
AND GIVING SELFLESSLY,
SPREADING JOY AND BEING THANKFUL
FOR OUR LOVING FAMILY."

HE LOOKED AT MUMMY WITH EYES OPEN WIDE
DEEP DOWN HE ALWAYS KNEW.
"THANK YOU FOR TELLING ME THE TRUTH ABOUT
SANTA, MUMMY."

"I LOVE YOU."

THERE IS ONE MORE THING
THAT'S REALLY IMPORTANT TO KNOW.
DIFFERENT FAMILIES HAVE DIFFERENT TRADITIONS
AND YOU'LL SEE THIS AS YOU GROW.

SOME FAMILIES LIKE TO PRETEND
THAT SANTA IS TRULY REAL.
EVERYONE GETS TO MAKE THEIR OWN CHOICE
SO BEING RESPECTFUL OF THIS IS A BIG DEAL.

NOW OUR STORY COMES TO AN END
BUT THERE'S ONE MORE ORDER OF BUSINESS
AND THAT IS FOR US TO WISH YOU A....

MERRY
CHRISTMAS

Made in United States
Orlando, FL
27 December 2024

56626857R00018